Iktomi
and the
Ducks

Orchard Books   New York

Also by Paul Goble:
Iktomi and the Boulder
Iktomi and the Berries

There goes that white guy,
Paul Goble, telling another
story about me. . . .
My attorney will Sioux.

Iktomi
and the
Ducks

a Plains Indian story

retold and illustrated
by PAUL GOBLE

for Janet and Robert, with all my love

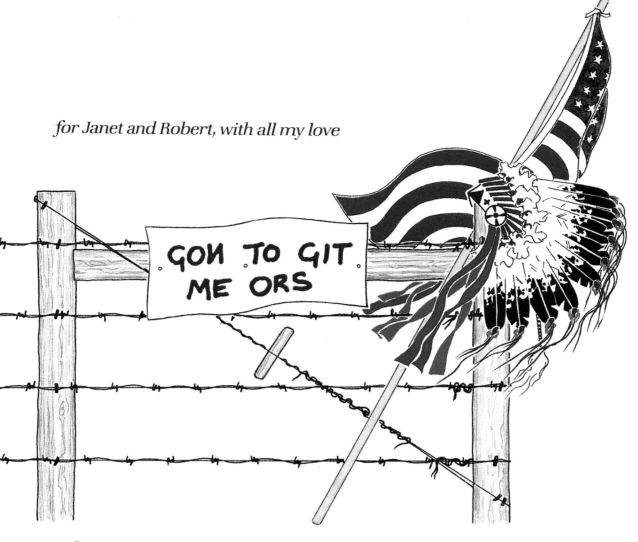

References

Ella C. Deloria, *Dakota Texts*, vol. 14, Publications of the American Ethnology Society, New York, 1932; George Bird Grinnell, *By Cheyenne Campfires*, Yale University Press, New Haven, 1926; *Blackfoot Lodge Tales*, Scribner's, New York, 1892; A. L. Kroeber, *Cheyenne Tales*, vol. XIII, *The Journal of American Folk-Lore* (1900); DeCost Smith, *Red Indian Experiences*, George Allen and Unwin Ltd., London, 1949; Henry Tall Bull and Tom Weist, *Ve'ho*, Montana Reading Publications, Billings, 1971; James R. Walker, *Lakota Myth*, University of Nebraska Press, Lincoln, 1983 (recorded c. 1900); Clark Wissler, *Some Dakota Myths*, vol. XX, *The Journal of American Folk-Lore* (1907); Zitkala-Sa, *Old Indian Legends*, Ginn, Boston, 1901.

Copyright © 1990 by Paul Goble. First Orchard Paperbacks edition 1994. All rights reserved. No part of this book may be reproduced or transmitted in any form or by any means, electronic or mechanical, including photocopying, recording, or by any information storage or retrieval system, without permission in writing from the Publisher. Orchard Books, 95 Madison Avenue, New York, NY 10016. Manufactured in the United States of America. Printed by Barton Press, Inc. Bound by Horowitz/Rae. Book design by Paul Goble. The text of this book is set in 22 pt. Zapf Book Light. The illustrations are India ink and watercolor, reproduced in combined line and halftone. Library of Congress Cataloging-in-Publication Data Goble, Paul. Iktomi and the ducks : a Plains Indian story / retold and illustrated by Paul Goble.   p.   cm. "A Richard Jackson book" - Half t.p. Includes bibliographical references. Summary: After outwitting some ducks, Iktomi, the Indian trickster, is outwitted by Coyote. ISBN 0-531-05883-2 (tr.)   ISBN 0-531-08483-3 (lib. bdg.)   ISBN 0-531-07044-1 (pbk.) 1. Indians of North America—Great Plains—Legends.   [1. Indians of North America—Great Plains—Legends.]   I. Title.   E78.G73G63   1990   398.2'08997—dc20   [398.2]   [E]   89-71025   10   9   8   7   6   5   4   3   2   1

About Iktomi

Stories about the trickster, Iktomi (*eek-toe-me*), belong to a category which Lakota people call *ohunkaka*: amusing stories which are not meant to be believed, but which often have moral lessons wrapped up inside them. In the old days they were only told after the sun had set.

All Native American people have the same trickster character. He goes by different names, but the story themes of his ridiculous antics are shared. *Iktomi and the Ducks* has two themes which seem to be almost unrelated: killing the ducks while they dance with their eyes closed, and the trees rubbing together. When these themes were first recorded at the end of the nineteenth century, they were found in the oral literature of peoples from the Mackenkie River in the far north of Canada, south through the Plains, Great Lakes and Woodlands, almost to Mexico. Many variations have been woven, but the themes are always there. One imagines that they are very old. They seem like fragments of almost forgotten stories. Even the trickster himself seems fragmentary and contradictory, being both negative prankster, and divine being who helped the Creator order Creation. Ella Deloria has written: "To our minds, these stories are a sort of hangover, so to speak, from a very, very remote past, from a different age, even from an order of beings different from ourselves."

When Native Americans tell a story nowadays, nine times out of ten it will be about their trickster. Stories which never existed in Buffalo Days have been added to the repertoire. Iktomi is still alive, and yet he is in danger of being relegated to a merely whimsical and entertaining character. In former times he lived in people's minds; he was brought constantly into everyday conversation: people's characteristics, their insincerities, ambitions and vulgarities were humorously likened to those of Iktomi. He was always loved by children, but adults enjoyed him too.

A Note for the Reader

Stories about Iktomi have always been told with a lot of "audience participation," and so when the text changes to gray italic, readers may want to allow their listeners to express their own thoughts about Iktomi. Iktomi's thoughts, printed in small type, can be read when looking at the pictures.

Those who are familiar with trickster stories may know him by a different name: Saynday (Kiowa), Old Man Coyote (Crow), Napi or Old Man (Blackfoot), Wihio or Ve'ho (Cheyenne). Instead of "Iktomi," use the name you know best.

Iktomi was walking along. . . .
Every story about Iktomi
starts this way.

Iktomi was walking along.
He was looking for his horse.
He wanted to ride it in the parade.

I really do like myself.
I look like one of the old-timers.

I bet all the girls will
want to ride with me.

My otter fur (imitation) necklace

My red silk shirt

My beaded cuffs

My blanket

My tobacco bag

My trade-cloth leggings

My moccasins

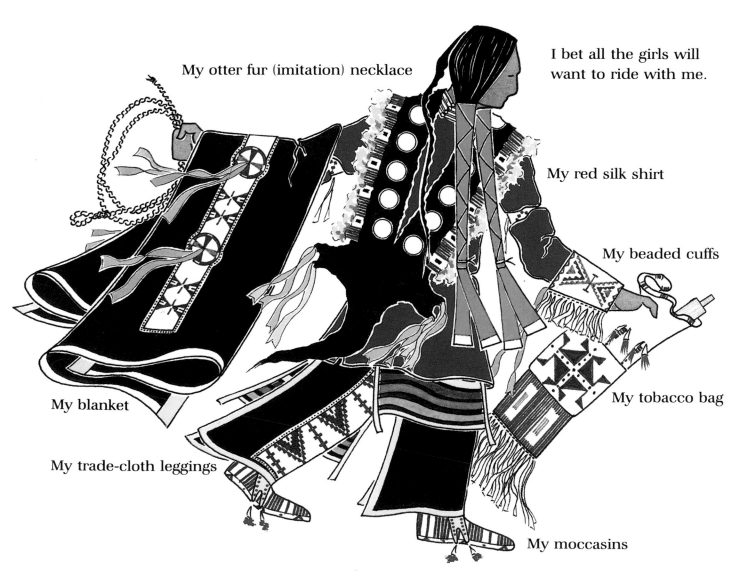

"I'm wearing my best clothes today,"
he thought to himself.
"I'll look magnificent on my horse."

Iktomi always thinks he is so great.

"I'll lead the parade.
Everybody will notice me.
'Look,' they'll say to their children,
'yonder rides our War Chief,
the bravest of the brave.' "

He thinks he is a chief,
but we know he's not, don't we?

Today I'm Sitting Bull.
Or am I Crazy Horse?

Iktomi walked and walked.
"Where has my horse gone?"
he wondered.
"I hope no white man has stolen him."

Can you see Iktomi's horse?

Iktomi looked this way . . .
and that way . . .
but he could not see his horse
anywhere.

*Who could possibly ride such a
wild horse?*

Iktomi noticed some ducks enjoying
themselves on a pond.
"Hmmmm . . . roast duck," he thought.
Iktomi is always thinking about food.
"Now, if only I could get hold of
those ducks. . . ."

I knew I was hungry.
I love duck roasted
on a campfire.

Ikto, you have such
brilliant ideas.

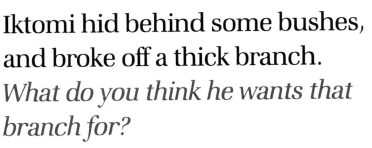

Iktomi hid behind some bushes,
and broke off a thick branch.
*What do you think he wants that
branch for?*

Iktomi spread his blanket on the ground.
He pulled up handfuls of grass
until he had collected a great pile.
He wrapped it, together with
the branch, inside his blanket.
Is that grass for his horse?

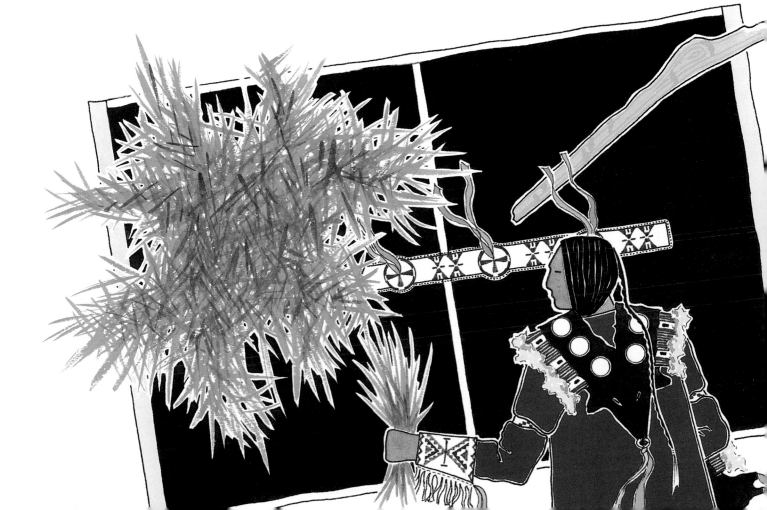

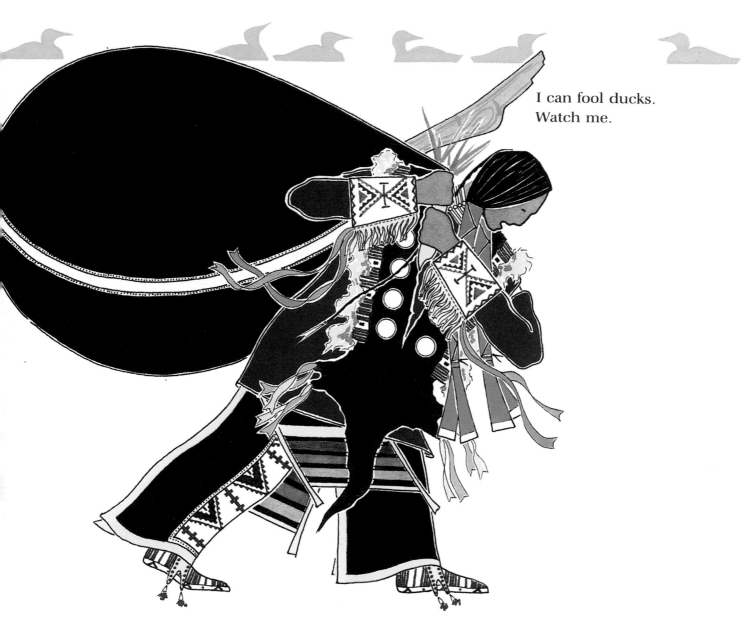

I can fool ducks.
Watch me.

Iktomi swung the bundle onto his back.

He walked briskly along the
edge of the pond with the enormous
bundle over his shoulders.
He pretended to be in a great hurry,
and to rub the sweat from his forehead.

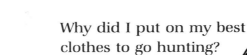

Why did I put on my best
clothes to go hunting?

The ducks were watching him.
"Hey! Ikto!" they called,
"What's that on your back?"
He walked on, pretending not to hear.

Iktomi is up to no good. . . .
What do you think he is plotting?

"Ikto! Stop! Talk to us!"
the ducks called again.
"What have you got in your blanket?"
"It's full of my latest songs,"
Iktomi replied.
"I just composed them.
I'm off to sing them at the pow-wow.
Everyone will want to dance to them."

Imagine carrying songs in a blanket!

"Sing us some, Ikto!" the ducks begged.
"Yes! Do sing us some!"
they implored him.
"Sorry," he said, "can't stop;
in a hurry to get to the pow-wow."
"Oh please, PLEASE," the ducks pleaded.

"Well . . ." he answered. "All right . . .
but only one."

Those quack-quacks will
believe anything I tell them.

The ducks swam to shore,
and waddled out onto the bank.
Iktomi felt inside his bundle,
and drew out a single blade of grass.
"I'll sing this one," he said.

Iktomi is up to mischief.
He is fooling the ducks, isn't he?

What else can I tell them?

Ikto, you are SO clever!
You can call ducks off
any pond!

Iktomi told the ducks: "Gather round,
and we'll all sing and dance together.
Now, this is a very special kind of song.
You must keep your eyes closed.
If you open them, they'll turn red.
I'll beat time on the ground
with my drumstick,"
and he pulled the branch
out of his bundle.
He calls that a drumstick!

"Close your eyes!" he told the ducks.
"Now, dance while I sing my song:
    Close your eyes
        and dance with me!
    Keep them shut
        or they'll turn red.
    Close your eyes
        and dance with me!"

You watch!
Now we'll really have
a pow-wow!!

Iktomi was beating time on the
ground with the branch:
      Thump-THUMP!
        Thump-THUMP!
          Thump-THUMP!
            Thump-THUMP!
"DANCE! Stamp your feet!"
Iktomi shouted.
The ducks joined in, eyes closed,
dancing with every bit of energy.

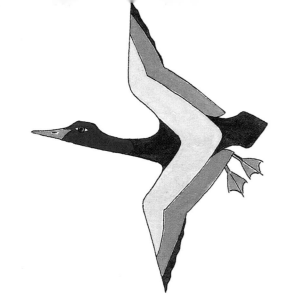

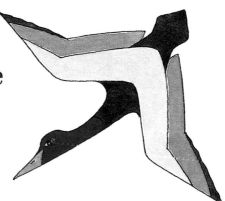

Suddenly, instead of beating time
on the ground, Iktomi started thumping
the ducks on their heads.
        Thump-THUMP!—a duck was dead.
        Thump-THUMP!—and another.
        Thump-THUMP!
                Thump-THUMP!
                        Thump-THUMP!

One duck opened the corner of an eye
—and saw what Iktomi was doing.
"Hey! Fly! IKTOMI IS KILLING US!"
All the ducks took to the air
in terror.

"Quack! Quack! Quack!"
Ducks can't dance to save
their lives.

Fantastic!
Look at that, Ikto!

Isn't Iktomi horrible?

*Have you noticed that some ducks
have red eyes?
They are the grandchildren of the duck
who peeked while dancing.*

Iktomi made a cooking fire.
He skewered the ducks on sticks
and put them around the fire to roast.
He buried one to bake in the ashes.
His mouth watered;
his stomach rumbled.

The wind started blowing.
The trees swayed from side to side.
Two trees creaked and scraped
against each other.
"Creak! Cre-e-e-e-e-e-e-eak!"
"Squeak! Sque-e-e-e-e-e-eak!"
The sound got on Iktomi's nerves.
"Brothers shouldn't argue,"
he told them.
"You must stop it, or I'll have to
come up and separate you."

Creak!

Scrape!

Scratch!

What a great hunter I am.

I can't stand the noise.
I might lose my appetite.

Oh dear . . . my ducks will burn.

When the trees took no notice,
Iktomi climbed up.
Just as he was pulling
the two trees apart,
the wind died, and he was trapped,
SQUASHED between them.
"What do you think you are doing?
Let go of me!" he demanded.
I AM IKTOMI!
I'll chop you down and cut you up."

He struggled and he squirmed.

Iktomi wriggled and he wrenched.
He hit and he kicked the trees,
but they held him prisoner.

*It looks like the end of Iktomi,
doesn't it?*

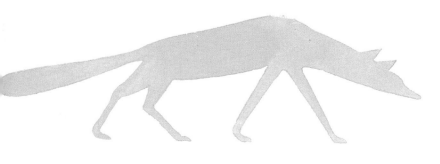

Oh help . . . poor me.
What am I going to do?

Now, Coyote had been watching everything.
You saw him, didn't you?

He trotted over to Iktomi's cooking fire.
"Go away!" Iktomi shouted.
"I won't give you anything."

That sneaky, beggarly,
deformed dog. . . .

When Iktomi saw that Coyote
had eaten all his roast ducks,
he pleaded:
"Leave me the one baking in the ashes.
That one's mine."
Coyote turned his back so Iktomi
could not see what he was doing.
He uncovered the duck which
Iktomi had buried in the ashes.
He filled it with red-hot coals,
and buried it again.

Coyote grinned and, licking his chops,
trotted on his way.

Water!
I must have water!

In a little while the wind blew again,
and the trees let Iktomi go free.

Iktomi dug the duck out of the ashes.
"Thank goodness—
Coyote left me the best one,"
he muttered.
He took a great hungry bite
—and got a mouthful of red-hot coals!!

"AHRRRRRRRRRRRRRR...............!!!"

He jumped up and down
spluttering and spitting ashes
in every direction.
Iktomi RAN toward the pond
and took a running jump ——————

I never liked roast duck—
too greasy—bad for my
cholesterol level.
Now, let me think:
WHAT was I going to do?

"Just wait until I catch up with
that thieving Coyote. . . .
I'll get even with him. Oh yes, I will!"
Dripping, Iktomi went on his way again.

*Iktomi has forgotten that he
was looking for his horse.
What do you think he
will get up to next?*